D0654428

With special thanks to Cherith Baldry
To James Noble –
the boy who would be Tom

www.beastquest.co.uk

ORCHARD BOOKS
338 Euston Road, London NW1 3BH
Orchard Books Australia
Level 17/207 Kent St, Sydney, NSW 2000

A Paperback Original
First published in Great Britain in 2007

Beast Quest is a registered trademark of Beast Quest Limited
Series created by Beast Quest Limited, London

A CIP catalogue record for this book is available
from the British Library.

ISBN 978 1 84616 482 8

35

Printed in Great Britain by CPI Group (UK) Ltd, Croydon, CR0 4YY

The paper and board used in this paperback are natural recyclable
products made from wood grown in sustainable forests. The
manufacturing processes conform to the environmental regulations of
the country of origin.

Orchard Books is a division of Hachette Children's Books,
an Hachette Livre UK company.

www.hachette.co.uk

Sepron
THE SEA SERPENT

BY ADAM BLADE

ORCHARD

THE ICY

THE

THE NORTHERN
MOUNTAINS

WESTERN OCEAN

THE FOREST
OF FEAR

T

Welcome to the kingdom of Avantia. I am Aduro – a good wizard residing in the palace of King Hugo. You join us at a difficult time. Let me explain...

It is written in the Ancient Scripts that our peaceful kingdom shall one day be plunged into peril.

Now that time has come.

Under the evil spell of Malvel the Dark Wizard, six Beasts – fire dragon, sea serpent, mountain giant, horse-man, snow monster and flame bird – run wild and destroy the land they once protected.

Avantia is in great danger.

The Ancient Scripts also predict an unlikely hero. It is written that a boy shall take up the Quest to free the Beasts from the curse and save the kingdom.

We do not know who this boy is, only that his time has come...

We pray our young hero will have the courage and the heart to take up the Quest. Will you join us as we wait and watch?

Avantia salutes you,

Aduro

PROLOGUE

The fishing boat rocked gently on the waves. Calum loosened the rope and let down the sail. His father began to cast out the net, hissing softly through his teeth as he worked.

"I don't know why we bother," he grumbled. "We haven't caught anything for a month!"

"You know what they say," Calum said. "The sea serpent has scared away the fish."

His father snorted. "Old wives'

tales! Anyway, I thought that sea serpent was meant to help us."

Calum glanced round, shivering slightly. Nothing broke the surface of the sea except for a small rocky island not far from the beach.

When they hauled in the net, there was nothing in it.

"Useless," his father said.

He cast the net out again. As Calum watched it sink into the depths of the water, he spotted something happening between the boat and the shore. It looked as if the sea was boiling. Then it began to churn angrily, and foam and waves dashed against the rocks.

"Look!" he cried, pointing. "Over there!"

His father turned, grabbing the side of the boat as it started to rock dangerously.

Then, out of the water rose a
monstrous head on a long, slender
neck. It was covered in thick,
rainbow-coloured scales and
barnacles. A golden collar round the
Beast's neck glinted in the sunshine,
and a glowing chain stretched from
this down into the water.

"What is it?" Calum's father yelled.

Calum scrambled for the rope to raise the sail, but it was too late. The Beast's neck arched and its vast head loomed over the boat. Calum stared up into huge, furious eyes that seemed to burn with cold fire. Choking with terror, he saw the creature's jaws gape open. Its long,

curving fangs snapped the boat's mast, and splinters showered down on father and son like rain.

Sea water slopped over Calum as the boat tilted. Cowering down, he wrapped his arms over his head and squeezed his eyes shut, as the roar of the sea serpent echoed all around him...

CHAPTER ONE

THE ROAD TO THE WEST

Tom brought Storm to a halt at the foot of a rocky slope. He and Elenna slid to the ground so that the horse could rest. Silver the wolf flopped down beside them, his tongue lolling out as he panted.

The hill where Tom had met and battled Ferno the Fire Dragon was far behind them. Now he and Elenna were heading west on the next stage of their Beast Quest.

Tom's heart began thumping again as he remembered how he had freed Ferno from the curse of Malvel the Dark Wizard. The dragon had burnt crops all over Avantia and blocked the river, making the land dry and barren. When Tom had unlocked the magic collar that imprisoned him, the dragon was released from the spell. As he flew away, he had dislodged the stones damming the river, and a foaming torrent had gushed down the hillside.

"I'll never forget how Ferno broke the rocks with his tail," Elenna said, as if she guessed what Tom was thinking. "Or how you leapt up on his wing! That was really brave."

"It wouldn't have worked if you hadn't shot that arrow up to me, with the key tied to it," Tom replied, feeling embarrassed by Elenna's praise. "I'd never have unlocked the collar without that."

"What you did was still the bravest thing I've ever seen," Elenna insisted.

"We both freed Ferno," Tom said firmly. "And now Avantia has water again."

"Yes, and no more burnt crops," Elenna agreed.

Silver leapt up again with an impatient yelp.

Elenna turned to Tom, a determined look in her eyes. "We'd better push on," she said.

Tom could still hear the words of Wizard Aduro ringing in his ears. Freeing Ferno the Fire Dragon was only the first of his tasks. Malvel's curse had turned the good Beasts of Avantia into evil monsters that were destroying the kingdom. It was Tom's Quest to free all the Beasts and save his people. Tom wasn't sure he could succeed. There was so much he had to do and so many Beasts to conquer! But he meant to try, with all the strength and courage he had. *While there's blood in my veins*, he thought, *I will not give up*.

This was the adventure Tom had been waiting for all his life. And even though his father, Taladon the Swift, had disappeared when Tom was a baby, he was determined to make him proud.

"Let's have another look at the map," he said.

He pulled out the scroll that Wizard Aduro had given him. On it a path glowed green, winding through hills and woodland until it reached the sea in the west.

As Tom looked at the map, a tiny head reared out of the waves drawn on the paper, just beside a spike of rock that looked like an island. A jagged tail slapped down, sending spray high into the air. Tom started as a drop splashed onto his hand.

"There's Sepron," said Elenna. Her voice was filled with awe.

"I still can't believe it!" said Tom. "A sea serpent!"

"It's angry." Elenna's eyes were wide, as if she had just realised the huge mission facing them. "How do you think it is destroying Avantia?"

"I don't know," Tom said, then he added boldly, "But whatever it's doing, we're going to stop it. That's part of our Quest."

Silver let out another loud yelp. He grabbed the corner of Elenna's cloak in his teeth and tugged gently. At the foot of the slope, Storm scraped one hoof impatiently on the stones.

Tom laughed. "All right, I know. It's time we were going."

He checked the map one last time and stowed it away in his pocket. Before he scrambled back onto Storm, he made sure that the shield Wizard Aduro had given him was firmly strapped to his back. It had been scorched by Ferno, but one of the dragon's reddish-black scales shone in its slot on the shield's surface. Was it true, Tom wondered, that the shield could now protect them from fire?

He swung himself into the saddle. Elenna sprang up behind him and wrapped her arms round his waist. Tom patted Storm's glossy black neck.

"On to the west!" he cried.

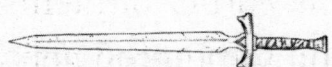

At first the path zigzagged up the slope, then through a belt of trees. By the time the sun went down they had reached a pass that curved through a range of low hills.

Tom stopped beside a pool and slid to the ground. "This would be a good place to make camp."

Elenna helped him to unsaddle Storm so the horse could drink from the pool. Silver stood beside him, lapping thirstily. Tom scooped a handful of cool water into his mouth then started to collect sticks for a fire.

"I'm starving!" said Elenna. "I'll see if there are any nuts or berries on these bushes."

While she was searching, Storm cropped the grass beside the path.

"We've nothing for Silver to eat," said Tom.

"He'll find something for himself," Elenna replied. "Go on, boy." She patted the wolf and shooed him away.

Silver waved his tail and vanished among the rocks. He returned before Tom and Elenna had finished eating, and they all settled down for the night.

Tom looked up at the stars, thinking about Sepron. He hoped they could reach the coast soon, before the sea serpent had the chance to harm the kingdom further.

They set off again early the next morning, and soon reached the edge of the hills. A long, smooth slope was in front of them. Far ahead Tom could make out the distant glimmer of the sea and a tiny rocky island.

"We're almost there!" Elenna exclaimed.

A flash of light on the water caught Tom's eye. He gasped.

"What's the matter?" Elenna asked.

"I'm not sure...but I think I saw Sepron."

He felt Elenna's grip on him tighten. "Where?"

"Over there, near that island." Tom pointed. "But he's gone now."

He dug his heels into Storm's side to urge him on. Soon the path levelled and they rode through farmland. Everything seemed deserted. Great patches of ground were covered in burnt stubble.

"Look!" Elenna cried, pointing to the blackened timbers of what had been a farmhouse. "Ferno has been here."

A shiver ran through Tom, even though he knew the dragon was now free from Malvel's evil spell and would never blast the land with fire again. He urged Storm to a faster trot, eager to keep moving. Silver

bounded a few paces ahead.

Suddenly, Storm reared. His forelegs pawed the air.

Elenna squealed in alarm and gripped Tom to stop herself sliding off.

"Storm – steady!" Tom yelled.

When the horse's forelegs fell to the ground he began skittering to one side. Tom tugged on the reins but couldn't get him under control.

Then he noticed that Silver was standing still, his legs stiff and the bushy grey fur on his shoulders bristling. He began whining uneasily.

"Something's wrong," said Elenna. "Silver always knows."

Tom glanced back at Elenna, noticing the alarm in her eyes. He looked round but saw nothing, just empty fields. There was no sign of danger. But Silver was still whimpering and Storm was tossing his head, his eyes rolling in panic. Beads of sweat had broken out on his black coat.

"What is it, boy?" Tom was still struggling to keep the terrified horse on the path. "What's the matter?"

Silver let out a howl. He was staring straight ahead. Following his gaze, Tom thought he could make out something moving on the horizon. A silver line had appeared, stretching as far as he could see in both directions. Sunlight glinted on it and then Tom could see watery swells and peaks, which quickly grew bigger and bigger.

"Tom." Elenna's voice sounded as if she could hardly speak for fear. "It's a tidal wave!"

CHAPTER TWO

RACE AGAINST THE SEA

Tom froze.

"Tom!" Elenna tugged hard at his shoulder.

Wrenching on the reins, he brought Storm's head round and dug his heels hard into the horse's side. "Run!" he yelled.

Storm leapt forward like an arrow from a bow. Yelping fiercely, Silver raced along not far behind.

"Faster!" Elenna cried. "The wave's catching us."

Tom risked a glance over his shoulder. Now he could see a huge wall of water rolling closer. He couldn't believe how fast it was coming.

He bent low over the horse's neck. "Come on, Storm," he urged. "You can do it!"

The path led back towards the hills. Could they reach the higher ground before the wave crashed down upon them?

Glancing back again, he saw Elenna's face was white with terror. Her hair was whipped back by the speed of their flight. Beyond her the wave reared up, blotting out the sky. The hills where they would be safe seemed very far away.

Then Elenna tugged at Tom's shoulder again. "Over there!" she gasped, pointing to one side.

It was a ridge jutting out into the valley. Smooth slabs of rock, covered in a mossy carpet, stood high above the rest of the land. It might just be high enough for Tom and Elenna to escape the flood.

Tom pulled on Storm's reins and the stallion plunged away from the path. His hooves thundered across the blackened fields.

But the roar of the wave was getting louder. When Tom looked back, he saw murky green water rising in a smooth curve behind him. The top was beginning to curl over, edged with white foam.

Storm's pace slowed as he started to climb over the rough ground. Tom had to cling to the front of the saddle to keep his seat. Elenna's arms were so tight round his waist he could hardly breathe. He couldn't see Silver, though he heard the wolf howling.

The slope grew steeper still. Tom was terrified that Storm would slip back, into the oncoming wave.

"Faster!" he gasped.

The horse leapt upwards, his hooves clattering on bare rock as he fought for balance. Tom let out a roar of panic. If Storm fell, they would all die!

Then the wave hit the ridge and sea water crashed around them, surging up Storm's legs. Spray shot into the air, drenching them. Tom's eyes stung and he blinked to clear them.

With a last effort, Storm heaved himself onto a spur of rock, while the wave licked hungrily just below. Tom and Elenna slid to the ground.

Storm was sweating and trembling.

Tom patted his neck. "Well done, boy. You saved us. You're the bravest—"

"Where's Silver?" Elenna's cry interrupted him.

Tom looked out over the stretch of churning water. Branches and other debris lurched past him. But there was no sign of the wolf.

"Silver! Silver!" Elenna called frantically.

Urgent yapping answered her. Tom spotted a dark shape thrusting through the waves. Silver was paddling furiously towards them. His muzzle vanished under the swirling water, then reappeared. Tom couldn't tell if he was making any headway.

"He can't do it! He'll drown!" Elenna sobbed.

She began tugging off her boots, ready to plunge into the water and grab the wolf.

Tom clutched her arm. "No – it's too dangerous!"

Before Elenna could struggle free, a surge of water tossed Silver closer. His paws thrashed, pushing him up to the rock. With a gasp of relief Elenna knelt on the edge to lean over and grab him by the scruff of his neck, helping him to safety.

Silver was panting hard, and water streamed off his thick coat. "You're safe!" Elenna cried. She threw herself down beside the wolf and hugged him fiercely. "We're all safe!"

"Only for now," Tom said. "I'm sure I saw the sea serpent from the top of the hill. It must have caused the tidal wave. If we don't free it from Malvel's curse, it'll flood the whole kingdom."

Tom touched the sword in his scabbard. He would free Sepron – whatever it took!

CHAPTER THREE

STRANDED!

Tom pulled the map out of his pocket again. The glowing green path that had led to the shores of the Western Ocean now ended in lapping waves. The tiny figure of Sepron had vanished.

Rolling up the map, Tom looked round. In front of him water stretched as far as he could see. Behind, a rough slope led up to the top of the ridge. A couple of twisted thorn trees stood out against the sky.

"Maybe we can get back into the hills," Elenna suggested. "There must be a way."

Tom pointed to the top of the ridge. "We should be able to see from up there."

With Elenna beside him he climbed the slope. When they reached the thorn trees they stopped in horror.

"No!" Elenna exclaimed.

They were standing on the highest part of the ridge. The lower part, which joined it to the range of hills beyond, had disappeared under the wave. They were now on an island surrounded by a vast lake.

Elenna folded her arms. "Now what do we do?"

Tom gazed towards the west. Out to sea he could see the rocky island jutting from the water. That must be where he had seen Sepron on the map. But without a boat they had no way of getting there.

"What's that?" Elenna pointed to a clump of trees on the opposite side of the ridge.

Behind the trees Tom could make out the grey walls of buildings, and he caught a glimpse of movement. "There's someone there," he said. "Maybe it's a farm."

"Let's go and see," Elenna suggested. "Whoever it is might be able to help us."

"Good idea. But we mustn't say anything about Sepron. The Quest is a secret."

They went back down the slope to collect Silver and Storm. Tom led the tired horse up the ridge and down the slope beyond to the clump of

trees on the other side. Elenna
followed with Silver at her heels.

As they approached the trees, Tom
saw groups of people clustered round
a few stone cottages. Lower down
the slope, more cottages were partly
covered by water. Waves lapped at
their windows. Beyond them, Tom
could see only thatched roofs, then
nothing but unbroken sea.

Elenna's eyes widened with shock.
"It's a village!" she exclaimed. "The
water has covered most of it."

"I hope no one was drowned," said Tom, as they approached the water.

At the sound of Tom's voice, a red-haired boy standing at the water's edge turned. "No, everyone's safe, thank goodness," he said.

"We're all lucky to be alive," Elenna said, then added, "I'm Elenna, and this is Tom."

"My name is Calum," said the boy. "Look at this!" He pointed at the flooded cottages. "What are we going to do now?"

"We'll stay and help," Elenna said.

Calum shook his head. "Thanks, but what good can anyone do? We can't live here any more. We'll have to move away, and it's all the fault of the sea serpent."

"The sea serpent?" Tom exclaimed, exchanging a startled glance with Elenna.

A man standing next to Calum said, "You'll think we're talking rubbish. I thought that myself once. But now I've seen the creature. It's out there. Legend says the serpent protects Avantia's fishermen and keeps the sea full of fish, but now it is doing just the opposite!"

Tom's stomach churned with excitement. They were in the right place. With a bit of luck he would soon be able to face Sepron and free him.

Calum gestured to the man. "My father and I were out at sea when we saw it," he explained. "It smashed the boat to pieces. I thought we would drown for sure."

"What did you do?" Elenna asked.

"We hung on to scraps of the wreckage and swam ashore," Calum replied. "Every minute I thought the sea serpent would swallow me."

"And that wasn't the first bit of trouble, either," his father added. "For weeks before that, we caught next to no fish. And now we have no boats. A fine lot of fishermen we are without boats!"

"There's one over there." Tom pointed to a small boat lying not far from the edge of the water.

"It's the only one left," said Calum despairingly. "And it's got a hole in it."

"I'll help you mend it if you like,"

Elenna offered. "My uncle's a fisherman, too, and he taught me how to do repairs."

Calum's father shook his head doubtfully, but a spark of hope appeared in the boy's eyes.

"Let us mend it, Father," Calum said. "At least it's something to do. We shouldn't give up hope yet."

The man nodded slowly. "All right." Then he walked to the water's edge and stood gazing at the sea, as if waiting for the serpent to return.

Tom wished he could reassure the fisherman. As soon as the boat was mended, he and Elenna could row out and find Sepron. But he couldn't tell anyone about his Quest or about the Beast being under an evil spell!

"We need wood for a fire," Elenna said. "And rope and tar to mend the hole."

Calum glanced round. "There's wood and rope scattered all over. And I'll find you some tar." He ran to one of the cottages and vanished inside.

While Elenna started to collect scattered pieces of driftwood, Tom unsaddled Storm and led him to the trees where there was grass for him to eat. He noticed a long branch lying under the trees and dragged it back with him. Then he found some scraps of rope by the water's edge, and began to unravel them.

Calum came back with a burning log from the cottage. A small girl with red hair trotted behind him, holding a pot of tar.

"This is my sister," he said. "She wants to help."

"Hello." Elenna smiled at the little girl and started the fire with the log Calum had brought.

Calum and his sister brought armfuls of bigger branches and laid them on the fire. They crackled in the flames, and smoke billowed into the air.

When Tom had finished unravelling the rope, he and Calum turned the boat over so that they could reach the jagged hole in the side. Tom noticed that the oars were lashed together under the seat. They were lucky. A boat without sail or oars wouldn't be much use.

Tom packed the strands of rope into the hole while Elenna put the pot on the fire and found a stick to stir the tar. When it was bubbling she grabbed the pot handle in a fold of her shirt and carried the pot over to the boat. Quickly she used a scrap of driftwood to plaster the hot tar over the rope strands, inside and out. Everyone gathered round to watch, and Silver whined in approval.

Suddenly Tom heard the fire roaring louder and felt a fierce heat on his back. Silver let out a terrified howl.

Tom turned to see Calum's sister piling more wood onto the fire. The green branches were spitting and crackling as the flames took hold.

"No, stop!" Tom shouted.

The little girl stumbled away from the fire. But it was too late. Flames billowed and the branches hurled out bubbles of hot resin. A spark fell on the pile of branches next to the fire, and more sparks shot into the air. One landed just beside the boat. Calum stamped hard on it to put it out.

But it was no use. The fire was out of control and creeping across the ground towards them!

CHAPTER FOUR

FIRE AND WATER

Tom looked desperately for his shield. Where had he left it? Then he spotted it at the water's edge where he had put it when he unsaddled Storm. He grabbed it and yelled to the others, "Get away from the fire! I'll make sure it doesn't get to the boat!"

Elenna and the others ran to a safe distance and watched as Tom flung his shield up before the fire, standing as close to it as he dared, with the boat not far behind him. Hot resin spat angrily as flames licked the shield. The heat from the fire singed the hair on Tom's arms, and he could barely hold the shield in place.

"Tom!" Elenna yelled. "It's not safe! Run!"

"No!" Tom shouted. "I'm sure I can hold the fire back!" He turned his face away to protect his eyes from the glare of the angry red flames. His tunic was damp with sweat.

Gradually, the blast of flame grew weaker. Still holding the shield before him, Tom dragged some of the branches away and the fire began to die down. Black smoke curled into the air.

At last Tom lowered the shield. "Is anyone hurt?" he asked.

Elenna and Calum shook their heads.

The little red-haired girl burst into tears. "I was only trying to help!"

Her father rushed up and hugged her. "It's all right," he said. "There's no harm done." To Tom he said quietly, "It's a good thing the ground was wet from the tidal wave, so the fire couldn't spread too quickly."

Tom looked round. The earth was scorched and steaming. That fire could have spread not only to the boat but to the cottages, and then... It didn't bear thinking about. He glanced over to the clump of trees where Storm was standing – thank goodness the horse had been out of harm's way.

Tom examined his shield and the gleaming reddish-black dragon scale in its scorched surface. Wizard Aduro had been right. Ferno's gift really was a protection against fire!

Looking up, Tom saw Calum and his father staring thoughtfully at the shield, then at him. Tom's stomach lurched. What would he say if they questioned him?

"Let's go back to the cottage," Calum said to his sister, patting her on the shoulder.

Silver raced back along the shore and threw himself at Elenna, who put her arms round the wolf's neck and hugged him.

"Is he all right?" Tom asked.

"Yes, he's fine. He wasn't anywhere near the fire." Scrambling to her feet, Elenna gestured towards Calum's father, who was examining the repair to the boat. "Let's ask if we can borrow the boat."

Tom nodded doubtfully. Would the fisherman be willing to lend them the boat? After all, Tom couldn't tell him the real reason he wanted to borrow it, or how urgent his Quest was. But there was no other way to reach Sepron. And Tom had to save the kingdom!

He walked up to the man. "Sir," he began politely, "may we borrow the boat? We'll take good care of it."

The fisherman straightened up. "This is the only boat we have left. Do you think I'm going to give it to you when we need it ourselves?"

"We'll leave Silver and Storm here

with you," Elenna said, coming to stand beside Tom. "That way you can be sure we'll bring the boat back."

The man shook his head. "I'm not calling you thieves. But anything could happen. There could be another wave, or a storm. And the sea serpent's still out there. You might drown, and we'd never see our boat again."

"But—" Tom protested.

"I'm sorry. The answer's no."

He turned and walked away. Tom stared after him in frustration. Without a boat, how could they get out to sea and free Sepron?

Elenna spoke close to his ear. "If he won't lend us the boat, we'll just have to borrow it without permission."

Tom stared at her. "What? We can't do that!"

"But we'll bring it back. Tom, you know that there'll be more tidal waves if we don't free Sepron from Malvel's spell. And there'll be no fish in the sea, either. These people will starve. We'll be taking the boat for their own good."

Tom thought carefully. Should he risk offending Calum's family? Or see the whole kingdom of Avantia destroyed by Malvel's curse? He knew he didn't have a choice.

"We'll take the boat and row out at dawn," he said.

CHAPTER FIVE

ON WITH THE QUEST

Tom and Elenna slept on the floor of one of the cottages with some of the villagers. Tom chose a spot near the door, so he and Elenna could sneak out without disturbing anyone.

He woke to feel Elenna shaking him by the shoulder.

"Come on!" she whispered. "It's time."

Faint grey light was leaking through the shuttered window into the cottage. Tom rose to his feet, careful not to make a noise, and edged open the door. He and Elenna crept outside.

The sky was growing pale above the trees. Tom could make out the dark shape of Storm, grazing further up the hill. Silver came bounding out of the trees and snuffled at Elenna's hand.

"Sshh, boy," she murmured.

Tom saw that the flood water had almost disappeared during the night. More of the cottages had appeared. The boat was where they had left it, but now it lay at the top of a long slope covered with debris.

"Oh, no!" Elenna's eyes were wide with shock. "How will we get the boat down to the water?"

The boat was small, but it was strongly built. Straining together, Tom and Elenna could barely lift it.

"This is no good," Tom panted, setting it down again. "If we could find some rope we could tie it to Storm and let him drag it."

"No!" Elenna protested. "Look how rocky the slope is. We'd risk smashing another hole in it."

Tom gazed down at the boat. They were so close, but without a boat they would never be able to reach Sepron.

"One more try," he said to Elenna. "We've got to shift it."

They both stooped down and gripped the upturned boat at the bow and stern. Then a shout came from the cottage they had left.

"Hey! What do you think you're doing?"

Tom let go of the boat and straightened up. Calum was coming out of the cottage. He strode towards Tom and Elenna.

Tom ran to meet him. "Calum, don't wake everyone, please. We can explain."

Calum's face was dark with anger. "I thought you wanted to help us. Now it looks as if you're trying to steal our boat."

"We only want to borrow it," Elenna pleaded.

"My father said no!"

Tom hesitated. To his relief, none of the other villagers had been disturbed by Calum's shout. If only he could persuade Calum... But he knew that he shouldn't tell anyone about his Beast Quest. That would only spread panic.

"I need the boat for something

really important," he began.

Calum was giving him a thoughtful look now. It was the way he had looked at Tom's shield after it had turned aside the flames. Then he glanced out to sea. "I think I can guess," he said. "I thought there was something strange when I saw what you did with your shield." He paused, then added, "You remind me of someone."

"Who?" Tom asked.

"A man who rode through here – oh, more than a year ago now. He looked just like you."

Tom's heart began to thump painfully. Could it have been his father? "What was his name?" he asked, gripping the boy's shoulders.

Calum shook his head. "He didn't say. He just told us he was on a Quest." He paused then said, "I think you might be on a Quest, too."

Tom was sure that the stranger must have been his father, Taladon. He ached to know more about him. He wanted to ask about every detail of his stay in the village, but there was no time. The sky was growing brighter – soon the villagers would be up and about. And he couldn't tell Calum his secret, even though he had almost guessed it for himself. He

held the boy's gaze steadily. Elenna didn't say a word, though Silver whined softly.

After a moment, Calum gave a brisk nod. "All right. I'll help you move the boat."

The three of them managed to lift the boat and carry it down the hill. With the flood water almost gone, they waded across a pebbly beach until the sea was deep enough to

launch the boat. Tom and Elenna scrambled on board. Silver yelped eagerly and tried to follow.

"No, boy," Elenna said, ruffling the thick fur round his neck. "You can't come this time."

"I'll look after him," Calum promised. "And your horse." He rested his hand on Silver's head. The wolf looked up at him and let out a mournful whine.

"We'll be back soon," Tom said.

Elenna gave Silver a last pat. Then she unlashed the oars and gave one to Tom. They began rowing out to sea.

Back on the beach, Calum stood knee-deep in water, with Silver at his side. He raised a hand. "Good luck!" he called.

"Thanks," Tom muttered, looking at Elenna. "We're going to need it."

CHAPTER SIX

DISCOVERY ON THE ISLAND

Rowing was hard work. Sweat plastered Tom's tunic to his body. His hands tingled from gripping the oar. Elenna's hair clung to her face, and she snatched a moment to wipe her forehead with her sleeve.

An eerie silence surrounded them. The only sounds were the creaking of the oars and the slap of their blades on the water. As they headed out to sea the water became choppy. A current seized the boat and it became harder to row.

Tom's muscles strained as he thrust the oars deep into the churning water. They had to keep going! He squeezed his eyes shut and tried to ignore the screaming pain of his muscles. He could hear Elenna panting with the effort.

Gradually Tom realised that he could make out the shape of a rocky island in the misty dawn light. "Let's head over there," he told Elenna. "I think that's where I saw Sepron, just before the tidal wave."

He looked over his shoulder, peering into the mist. There was no sign of the sea serpent. Tom felt an icy shiver down his spine as he thought of the great head rising out of the water.

Then Elenna let out a cry. "Tom! The boat's leaking!"

Tom started. Water was washing round his feet and more was oozing through the repair Elenna had made the day before. He was so wet from launching the boat that he hadn't noticed.

"The tar hasn't had time to set properly," Elenna said. "We'll have to beach the boat and fix it."

"We can't go back to the village!" Tom said, alarmed.

"Give me your oar. I'll row while you bail. We'll try to land on the rocky island."

Elenna started to row again while Tom cupped his hands and bailed out the water.

The island gradually grew closer, and Tom spotted a narrow strip of

pebbles between two spiky crags.
"There!" he exclaimed.

The water swirled dangerously
round the rocks as Elenna rowed
between them, struggling to keep the
boat on a steady course. The boat

lurched and rocked in the waves. But at last Tom felt the bottom scrape against the pebbles. Puffing out a grateful sigh, Elenna pulled the oars into the boat. Then they both leapt out and dragged the boat out of the water.

While Elenna packed the rope and tar more firmly into the hole, Tom scooped the rest of the water out of the bottom of the boat. When he had finished, he walked down to the water's edge and scanned the sea. The surface shone silver in the growing light of morning, and was ridged with waves that burst into foam as they hit the rocks.

"Where are you, Sepron?" Tom wondered.

"There!" Elenna said at last. "That should hold it until we get back to shore."

Tom knew that by now the sun
must have risen over the hills inland.
But the sea mist seemed suddenly to
have grown thicker and he couldn't
see the land. The water level had
sunk even further. More of the rocks
were exposed and seaweed lay
everywhere. Tom wrinkled his nose
at the smell. A silver fish was
flapping helplessly on a flat rock.
Elenna gave it a gentle push and it

flopped back into the sea.

"What now?" she asked, gazing round.

Tom pulled out the map and hastily unfolded it. "The map shows Sepron swimming in the water beside this island," he muttered. "He must be close." He looked back up at the sea. It was still quiet but beneath those waves Sepron was lurking. If that huge serpent burst through the surface

of the water now, Tom and Elenna wouldn't stand a chance. There was no point hanging about. They had to get out there and find the Beast!

"Let's take a look around," Tom suggested. "We might spot something that will show us where to find Sepron."

Together he and Elenna clambered over the rocky base of the island. There was nothing to see except more seaweed and tiny scuttling crabs. There had to be a clue somewhere! Then Tom spotted an iron hoop driven into the rock.

"Hey!" he called to Elenna. "Come and look at this."

Elenna hurried over to join him. Examining the hoop, Tom saw that a thick golden chain was fixed to it, leading down into the water. It was draped with seaweed and covered with barnacles, but it still gave off a mysterious glow, which faded as the chain sank deeper into the water.

Elenna caught her breath. "Do you think it's enchanted?"

Tom crouched down, touched the chain and nodded. "This must be what's trapping Sepron!" he said.

CHAPTER SEVEN

SEPRON AT LAST!

"You're right!" said Elenna. "This chain must lead to a golden collar like the one on Ferno."

"It's the only clue we have anyway," Tom replied. "We need to follow it. Let's fetch the boat."

Tom and Elenna pushed the boat back into the water. To Tom's relief, the new repair seemed to be holding and the bottom of the boat stayed dry.

They rowed round the rocks to where the iron ring was holding the chain. Then they pulled the oars into the boat. Tom and Elenna paused to look at each other. It was now or never.

Tom could feel the cold fist of fear in the pit of his stomach. He could see that Elenna felt scared, too. As her hand reached out for the chain, Tom could see it tremble. He put his own hand on top of hers.

"Don't worry," he said. "We'll be OK."

"Will we?" asked Elenna.

Tom tried to smile. Then he shook himself and pulled the chain up firmly.

"Heave!" he said, and the two of them started to pull on the golden chain, which was slippery from the seaweed that clung to it. Hand over hand, they followed the chain, as it pulled the boat out into the sea. The thick mist folded around them and soon the rocky island was out of sight. The surface of the sea was flat now, and all they could hear was the water splashing from the chain.

"Try not to rock the boat," Elenna said.

Tom nodded. It was best not to let Sepron know they were close until they were ready. But the chain was heavy.

"This is hard work!" Tom gasped.

Then the chain slipped through his hands and fell to the floor of the boat. The boat lurched and the water grew choppy. Elenna grabbed the side and peered down into the sea.

"There's something there!" she exclaimed. "Something huge."

Tom looked down beside her. Sure

enough, a vast, dark shadow was gliding underneath the boat. He froze at the sound of a loud splash.

Something had broken through the surface of the water on the other side of the boat. Huge drops of sea water rained down on him and Elenna.

Tom knew what he was going to see. Bracing himself, he glanced over his shoulder. Elenna screamed.

Rearing out of the sea was the huge head of the sea serpent. They were face to face with Sepron!

The Beast's eyes were huge and pale, flashing with icy anger. Shimmering scales in all the colours of the rainbow covered its head and neck, and sea water foamed all around it.

"It's beautiful!" Elenna whispered.

Tom felt a sudden stab of joy. For all the Beast's size and anger, it *was*

beautiful. It should have been allowed to roam freely in the sea, instead of being tethered here by evil magic.

"Look at its collar," Tom said, pointing. "You're right, it's locked just like Ferno's collar was."

A golden chain trailed from the collar down into the sea. Roaring, Sepron lashed his head to and fro, trying to free himself. Then he plunged back under the waves.

The surface of the sea rolled as he vanished, and the boat rocked dangerously. Tom and Elenna clung to the side until the water grew quiet again.

Tom peered down into the sea. He narrowed his eyes as an idea grew inside him. Sepron was down there, somewhere. But the serpent couldn't hide for ever. Tom knew what he had to do. He had to follow

him into its depths.

"I'm going in," Tom said. "If I can hold my breath for long enough, I should be able to unlock the collar with the key Wizard Aduro gave me." He pulled it out of his pocket and held it up.

Elenna gave him an anxious look, but didn't try to stop him. "Be careful," she said quietly.

"Don't worry, I will."

"There must be something I can do to help," Elenna said.

Tom picked up his shield and gave it to her. "Hold this so it reflects the sunlight on the water," he told her. "It'll help me find my way back."

Slipping off his boots and the jerkin that he wore as a shirt, Tom sat on the side of the boat. He stared down into the deep blue sea. "While there's blood in my veins," he muttered, "I cannot fail. I will free Sepron!"

He took a huge gulp of air. Then he dived into the water.

CHAPTER EIGHT

SEPRON'S KINGDOM

Tom struck out energetically. He was swimming in an eerie, silent world, where everything seemed to move more slowly. The water was dappled by sunlight breaking through from the surface. Silver bubbles of air streamed away from him.

As he plunged deeper the only sound he heard was the rushing in his ears. The sunlight faded and panic gripped him as he faced the dark depths. He would never be able to hold his breath for long enough. He would drown! He wanted to turn round and swim back to the light.

Then he forced himself to be calm. He couldn't turn back now. This was his Quest. No one else could help the fishermen and free the kingdom of

Avantia from the threat of Sepron.
He plunged deeper still with strong,
sure strokes.

Then he spotted a golden light. It
was Sepron's chain!

Tom swam towards it and followed
it down. It led through waving
fronds of seaweed, which glided
gently aside as Tom pushed through
them. Shoals of electric-blue fish

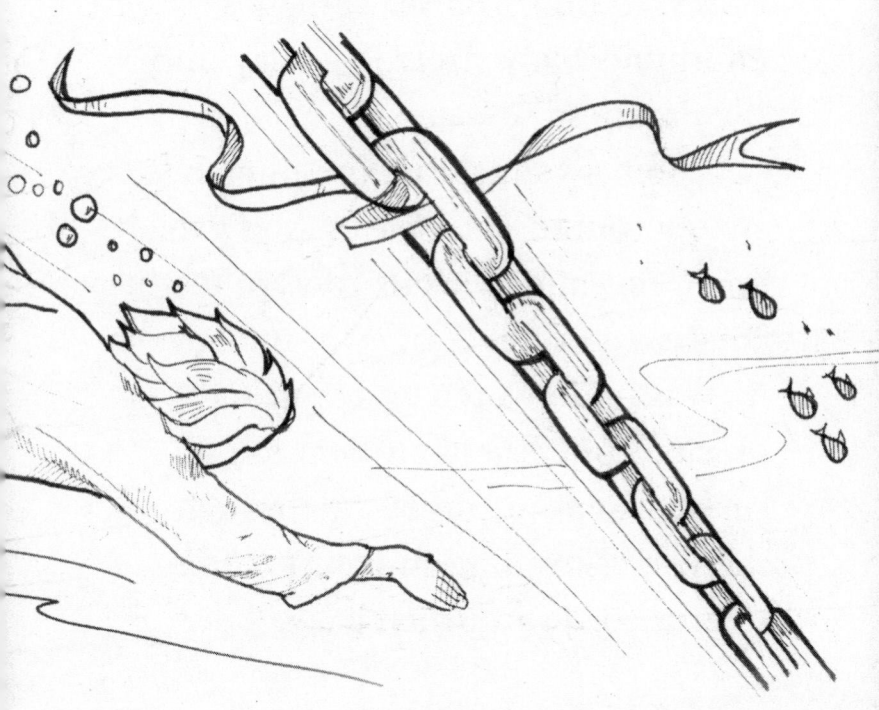

darted past Tom's face as he pulled himself deeper into the sea. The fish quickly swam out of sight, as if they knew what was about to happen. Further below, coral rose from the sea bed. Lying among the coral was Sepron.

Tom jumped and almost took a huge gulp of water. Sepron's head and the collar with the padlock were closest to him. The sea serpent's enormous body stretched away into the darkness.

As Tom swam closer, the huge head swung round. The Beast's jaws gaped open, revealing vicious rows of teeth. Tom cried out in fear, even though he was underwater, and watched precious bubbles of air float to the surface. Sepron surged up through the water, heading straight for Tom.

Terrified, Tom turned back. Arms

and legs pumping, he swam up to the light. The last of his air bubbled away. His lungs were hurting as he fought not to swallow water.

A bright spot on the surface showed Tom where to aim for. He glanced back, sure that Sepron's mighty jaws would snap shut on his legs at any moment. But to his relief he saw the sea monster give up the chase and sink back into the gloomy depths.

A moment later Tom's head and shoulders broke the surface. He trod water, desperately gulping in air. Sunlight dazzled him. When he could see properly he spotted the boat close by, with Elenna still holding up his shield. He had never been so glad to see anything in his life!

"Tom! Are you all right?" she shouted.

"Yes, fine," Tom panted. Though he

didn't feel fine. He was exhausted. But he already knew he was going to have to dive down again. He dragged his limbs through the water to Elenna and the boat. Could he really do it once more? "I have to!" he muttered to himself as he swam.

"Did you find Sepron?" Elenna asked.

Tom tried to ignore the bitter pang of disappointment as he admitted that he'd failed. "Found him, but..." Tom was still gasping for air, "...couldn't get close. Got to try again."

"Don't take in too much air," Elenna called. "And try to move slowly so you don't waste it."

Tom nodded, grateful for Elenna's advice.

He trod water until he could breathe easily again. Then he took

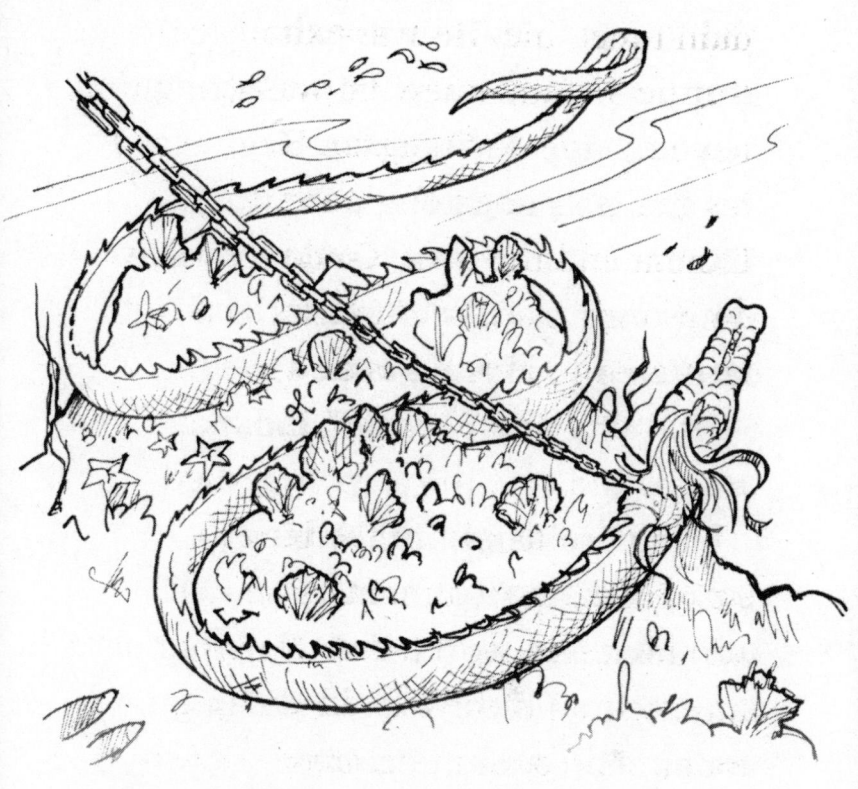

a last gulp of air, but not too much.
Waving to Elenna, he plunged
beneath the surface.

This time he found the chain more
quickly and followed it down to the
coral reef. Sepron was still lying
there, his coils wrapped loosely about
a spire of coral.

Cautiously, Tom swam closer, keeping behind a wall of rocks until he could approach Sepron from behind. He slid through the water, desperate not to disturb the serpent. When he was close enough, he darted forward and grasped the glowing collar with one hand.

Straight away, the serpent lashed its head back and forth, trying to shake him off. Tom clung grimly to the collar and worked his way round until he found the lock in the collar, under Sepron's jutting jaws.

As quickly as he could, Tom took Wizard Aduro's key from his pocket. He thrust it into the lock. But when he tried to turn it, the key stuck. Numb with horror, Tom realised this was a different kind of lock. The key was useless!

Sepron's head heaved upwards.

Tom lost his grip on the collar and rolled over helplessly in the surging water. One of the serpent's coils grazed his arm and knocked the key out of his hand. It glinted in the glow from the chain and sank towards the ocean floor. Tom watched it despairingly. There was no point in swimming after it. It wouldn't open the lock.

What can I do now? he thought. *How can I free Sepron without a key?*

CHAPTER NINE

THE LAST CHANCE

Sepron's neck curved round, his hungry jaws reaching for Tom. With failing strength Tom kicked out, driving himself back to the surface. His chest was bursting for air.

Once more he spotted the bright patch of sunlight from the shield Elenna held. Somehow he broke through the surface of the water near the boat, his mouth searching for air. Shaking wet hair out of his eyes, he gasped and panted.

"Tom!" Elenna cried. "Is everything all right? Is Sepron free?"

"No. The key didn't fit." Tom's voice was hoarse. He swam up to the boat and grabbed the side. "And then I dropped it. There's no way to get the collar off."

Elenna's eyes widened in horror. "What are we going to do?"

Tom's eyes fell on his scabbard. "I'll try this!" he said, unsheathing his sword.

Holding the blade out in front of him, Tom plunged down into the sea again. This time he sensed a massive shadow before he reached the bottom, and he realised that Sepron was waiting for him.

The serpent's neck arched over Tom and its sharp teeth closed inches from his foot as he swam deeper. But he couldn't outswim the Beast. He had to unfasten the collar!

His heart thumping, Tom knew he had to act now. His air wouldn't last long, and if he tried to resurface, Sepron would snap him up. *This is*

my last chance! he thought.

He turned in the water and drove himself towards Sepron's body. As the huge jaws gaped open Tom swam underneath them and grabbed the collar. Sepron's scaly head lashed to and fro, and Tom could hardly fit the tip of his sword in the lock.

By now he desperately needed air again. His arms and legs felt like lead and the sword was weighing him down as he struggled to turn the blade in the lock. *This has to work!* he told himself. *It has to*! He summoned all his strength, and tried one last time.

The lock sprang open with a mighty judder, throwing Tom backwards in the water. Instantly, Sepron stopped thrashing and the golden chain began to loosen. Impatient to be free, the serpent snapped at it angrily and tore the golden links apart with his gigantic teeth. The chain and collar glowed a fiery blue for a second, then disappeared. For so long, Sepron had been under Malvel's curse. But now the Beast was free!

CHAPTER TEN

THE NEXT QUEST

Tom made for the surface, dragging his sword through the water. His head throbbed with exhaustion and he could hardly move his arms and legs.

Then he felt something nudge him from below. Terror gripped him as he looked down into Sepron's face. But the anger had gone. The serpent's pale eyes shone joyfully. He gave Tom another nudge, pushing him up towards the light.

As Tom broke the surface, Sepron lifted him right out of the water. Tom clung to the Beast as it stretched its slender neck towards the boat.

"Tom!" Elenna cried out. "The collar's gone. You did it!"

Tom looked up and grinned. "Yes! Sepron is free!"

As the sea serpent lowered its head to set Tom down gently in the boat, something fell from its jaws. Tom picked it up.

"It's a tooth," he said, gazing at the jagged piece of ivory. He looked up at Sepron, but the serpent didn't seem to be in pain. It must have loosened the tooth when it tore at the golden chain. Tom reached up a hand and touched the Beast's shimmering scales. "Thank you," he said. He might have drowned without Sepron's help.

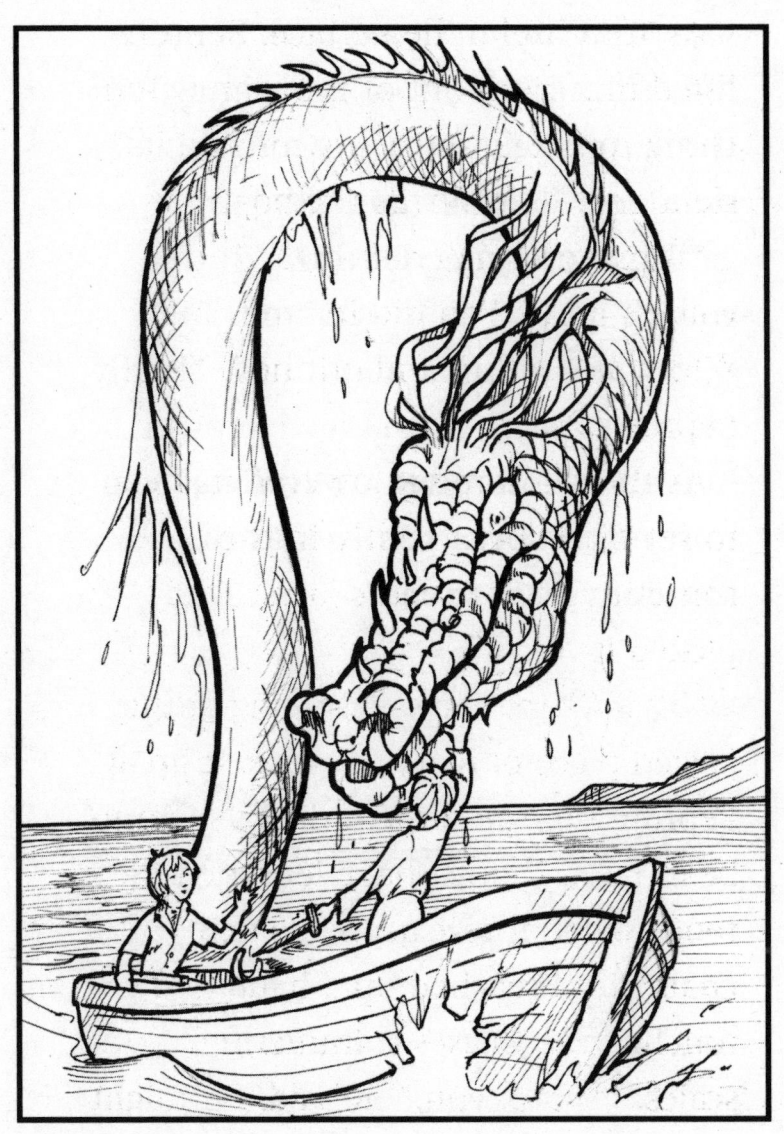

The Beast dipped its head in farewell. Then it dived back beneath the surface. Tom caught a glimpse of the serpent gliding away into the open sea. It was beautiful to see how gently Sepron moved through the waves; he was truly at home. Tom didn't like to think about how cruelly Malvel's spell had changed Sepron into an evil monster. Malvel was hurting the Beasts as well as the kingdom of Avantia.

"Sepron's free now," he said. "I think we're safe to say that there won't be any more tidal waves. And there will be fish in the ocean once again."

He and Elenna stared at each other for a moment. Then Elenna let out a whoop of triumph. She and Tom flung their arms round each other and hugged in excitement and relief.

Tom started at the sound of a polite cough just behind him. He and Elenna leapt apart. It was Wizard Aduro, who seemed to be standing on the waves close to the boat. But Tom could see the ocean through his robe. so he realised that this was another vision. Aduro was in the city of Avantia, but he had magically sent an image of himself so that he could talk to Tom and Elenna face to face. It was good to see him.

"Well done!" the wizard said. "I can

see I was right to choose you, Tom. You've freed Sepron from the evil spell and made the sea he protects safe again."

"I couldn't have done it without Elenna," said Tom.

Wizard Aduro smiled. "You have both shown great courage," he said. "All Avantia will be grateful to you. And now," he added, "is that a serpent's tooth that I see there?"

Tom held out the jagged piece. "Sepron dropped it in our boat."

"That tooth is a present from the serpent. Place it in the front of your shield," the wizard instructed him.

Tom picked up his shield. An empty slot glowing with sea-green light had opened up in his shield above Ferno's dragon scale. It shone more brightly as Tom fitted Sepron's tooth into it. Then the sides of the hole closed round the tooth as if the shield had been waiting for it all along.

"Now your shield will protect you from on-rushing water," Wizard Aduro said. "Not even the fiercest torrent will be able to harm you."

Tom gazed at the shield in wonder. He had already tested it against fire. Now it would protect him from water as well. "Thank you!" he said.

"Don't thank me," said Wizard Aduro, his eyes twinkling. "You won the tooth yourself. With each Beast that you free, your powers will grow."

Tom glanced at Elenna; her eyes were wide with wonder.

"What must we do now?" she asked.

"First, go back to the village," replied the wizard. "Tell your friend Calum that he and his family have nothing to fear now."

Tom nodded. "Yes. And we have to collect Storm and Silver."

"Then you must ride to the mountains in the north," Wizard Aduro continued. "Arcta the mountain giant is also under Malvel's curse and is threatening the kingdom."

"What's happening?" Elenna asked.

"Arcta is sending landslides onto the trading town at the foot of the mountains. If the town is destroyed, there will be no trade and the whole kingdom will suffer."

"And it's our job to stop him," Tom said. He could imagine rocks, mud and earth raining down on the town. The people there must be terrified.

"That's right," said Wizard Aduro. "Freeing Arcta is your next Quest."

"I'll do my best," Tom promised.

"The map will help you again," Aduro told him.

"Thank you. I—" Tom began. But Wizard Aduro's form had started to fade. The ocean shone more brightly through his robes. Then he was gone.

Tom felt a sudden pang of loneliness. He missed his uncle and aunt, and wondered again where his father was. But he had to continue with his Quest. He looked at Elenna. They had faced terrible danger together and survived. He knew they made a great team. Together, they would succeed in the Beast Quest.

"While there's blood in my veins, I'll free every one of the Beasts," he vowed.

Join Tom on the next stage
of the Beast Quest

Meet

ARCTA
THE MOUNTAIN
GIANT

Can Tom free Arcta from
Malvel's evil spell?

PROLOGUE

The caravan of wagons moved slowly along the high mountain road. As the road became steeper, the horses struggled to pull the wagons, which were loaded with food and supplies for the trading town in the mountains.

"How much longer?" a boy in the first wagon asked impatiently.

His father looked ahead at the narrow, winding road as it snaked up the mountain. It was a dangerous route, surrounded by trees, and rocks were scattered everywhere, as if there had been many landslides. "Be patient, Jack," he said. "Once we get to the pass, it's not much further." He pointed to a ridge in the distance.

Jack looked. Above the ridge, dark clouds were gathering, casting long shadows down the mountainside. The air began to cool as the sun disappeared behind the clouds.

As the wagons rounded a bend in the road, a fierce mountain wind hit them. The boy shivered and pulled his coat tighter.

"We'd better hurry if we're going to beat

this storm," Jack's father called to the other traders, his voice almost lost in the wind. "We don't want to get trapped here and freeze to death."

They pushed on. But the wind seemed to gain in strength and was soon screaming through the trees. Suddenly a thunderous crash echoed through the valley. The ground began to shake. All the wagons stopped, and the traders looked around in confusion.

"What was that?" one said.

Then they heard a deep rumbling sound and the loud crack of splintering wood, as if a tree were being snapped in half.

"What's happening?" Jack asked, trying to halt the panic in his voice.

His father looked towards the ridge. "I don't know, son," he said.

It was the first time Jack had seen fear in his father's eyes, and it sent shivers down his spine.

The ground now trembled so violently that it was hard not to fall off the wagons. The horses began to rear up, trying to escape from their harnesses. One wagon broke away and started to slide back down the mountain road, its contents spilling everywhere. Men dived out of the way as heavy barrels tumbled towards them. Then, in front of the wagons, huge boulders tore through the trees and crashed across the narrow road, just missing Jack and his father.

The road ahead was blocked!

The crashing grew louder.

Then, above them on the ridge, something appeared. In the chaos Jack was the only one to see it.

It was a giant Beast, as tall as the trees.

"Run!" Jack yelled. "Run for your lives!"

CHAPTER ONE

A NEW ADVENTURE

Tom and Elenna stopped at a fork in the road. The road to the east led towards the farms of Avantia. The road to the north would guide them into the kingdom's mighty mountains.

Tom knew which one they needed to take to find the next Beast in their Quest.

Sitting behind him on Storm, Tom's black stallion, Elenna hesitated. In the distance the mountain peaks were wrapped in dark, ominous clouds. She feared this mission was going to be even more dangerous than the last.

"Let's go, Elenna. We'll be all right," Tom said. Then, sensing his friend's nervousness, he added with a smile, "I mean, I've got you and the mutt for protection, haven't I?"

"The mutt? Well, thank you very much!" Elenna whistled to her pet wolf, Silver, who was sniffing some bushes nearby. "Come on, boy – let's teach our friend some manners!"

She pointed at Tom, and the wolf bounded across and playfully nipped his heels.

"Ow!" Tom cried.

"Take it back!" Elenna demanded.

"All right! All right! I take it back!" Tom laughed.

Elenna gave another short whistle. Silver immediately left Tom alone and trotted back to her side.

Tom smiled. They were in this together.

The four of them set out on the road to the north.

Before he'd met Elenna, Tom had been chosen by King Hugo and his royal adviser, Wizard Aduro, for this Quest. He was to save the kingdom of Avantia from Beasts who had been trapped by the evil spell of Malvel the Dark Wizard and were destroying the land. Tom's mission was to free them from the curse, so that they could protect Avantia once more.

He wished with all his heart that his father, Taladon the Swift, could see him as he took part in the biggest adventure of his life. But his father had disappeared when he was a baby, and Tom knew that wish would never come true.

Before the Quest, Tom thought the Beasts only existed in legend. But now that he had fought and freed two of them himself – Ferno the fire dragon and Sepron the sea serpent – he knew just how real they were, and how deadly they could be.

So far he and Elenna had only survived by working together. Now they had to face a new danger that lurked in the mountains of the north.

Arcta the mountain giant.

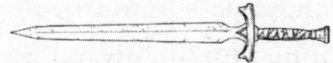

They travelled north through the foothills for some time, then Tom brought Storm to a halt. The trail before them led up a steep hill, surrounded by boulders and trees. "Let's check we're going the right way," he said. He fumbled for the magic map Wizard Aduro had given him and unrolled it. Pine trees and mountains rose up from the old parchment, standing as tall as Tom's thumbnail. The path they were following glowed.

"Another day's ride and we should reach the town," Elenna said, peering over his shoulder.

Tom looked closely at the map. The town was surrounded by five jagged mountains, and the road leading to it was long and winding. One part looked blocked by a landslide. He touched it and a plume of dust rose up from the map. They might have to find another way round. Tom had never tried to climb a mountain before. Would it be as steep and as dangerous as he imagined?

"We'd better make camp soon," he said. "We're going to need all our energy to get to up that mountain pass tomorrow."

They continued up the hill. At the top they stopped suddenly. Although they had seen the mountain peaks from a distance, now they could see the whole range. Mountains stretched as far as they could see. Dark shadows filled the folds and gullies, while the summits seemed to blaze in the late afternoon sun. Like rows of sharp teeth, the mountains stood out against the deep-blue sky.

"It's beautiful," whispered Elenna.

Tom nodded. He'd seen many things on his Quest so far, but no landscape as breathtaking as this.

Just then they noticed a ragged group of men coming down the trail towards them. Tom gripped his sword.

One of the men called out a greeting as they drew near. Tom could see he was carrying a young boy over his shoulder.

When the group reached them, Tom and Elenna saw that the men were traders. But they looked dirty and tired, and the boy appeared to be injured – his head was wrapped in a bloody strip of cloth.

"Can you help us?" the man carrying the boy asked. "Do you have any water? All our supplies have been destroyed."

Tom immediately passed him his water canteen. "What happened?"

"We were part of a trading caravan, bringing supplies to the town," the man explained, setting the boy down and giving him some water. "There was a landslide and we were lucky to survive."

"What triggered it?" asked Elenna.

"We don't know. The mountains are usually very stable. But the weather was odd and—"

"The giant…" spluttered the injured boy. "It was a giant…"

Tom and Elenna exchanged glances.

"Don't mind Jack," one of the men said quietly. "He got a bump on the head."

The first man said grimly, "I hope you two aren't going into the mountains."

"I'm afraid we are," said Tom.

"The mountains are dangerous, even in the best conditions," he warned, looking concerned. "The main road is blocked now and the weather's bad. I'd turn back. That's what we're doing."

"We don't have a choice," Tom said bravely.

"Well, if you must go, take this." The trader handed Tom a short length of rope. "It's not much, but it's all I have in return for your kindness. It may come in handy."

"Thank you," said Tom.

They gave the traders some more of their water and all the food they could spare, then said goodbye.

"Beware of the giant…" the young boy called back, as the traders made their way south.

Tom, Elenna, Storm and Silver pressed north. Soon the sky grew dark. It began to drizzle and the ground became muddy.

"We'd better hurry up and make camp," Elenna said. "We're going to get soaked."

Tom scanned the next hill and spotted an outcrop of rock that would provide shelter for the night. They began to climb towards it.

Just then Silver started to growl and his fur stood on end.

"What is it, boy?" Tom jumped off Storm and crouched beside the wolf. He looked all around but the hillside was deserted.

Elenna shivered, and Storm pranced nervously, his ears pricked up.

Then, quite suddenly, the horse halted, planting all four hooves firmly on the ground.

"Come on, Storm," Elenna said, touching her heels to his sides. "It's all right…" She stopped with a gasp.

Storm was slowly moving backwards down the hillside – even though he was standing still!

"Tom!" Elenna cried, as Storm started to slide more quickly. "The ground's not safe!"

"Jump off!" Tom yelled.

Storm fought to keep his balance but his hind legs slipped from under him. With Elenna clinging to his mane, the horse fell heavily onto his side. His hooves sent great clods of mud flying into the air, and Elenna crashed to the ground with a cry.

"Storm! Elenna!" Tom shouted, his voice

filled with panic.

Elenna's eyes were wide with fear as she pointed up the hill, past Tom.

"Mudslide!" she screamed.

Follow this quest to the end in ARCTA THE MOUNTAIN GIANT.

Win an exclusive
Beast Quest T-shirt and goody bag!

Tom has battled many fearsome Beasts and we want to know which one is your favourite! Send us a drawing or painting of your favourite Beast and tell us in 30 words why you think it's the best.

Each month we will select **three** winners to receive a Beast Quest T-shirt and goody bag!

Send your entry on a postcard to
BEAST QUEST COMPETITION
Orchard Books, 338 Euston Road, London NW1 3BH.

Australian readers should email:
childrens.books@hachette.com.au

New Zealand readers should write to:
Beast Quest Competition, PO Box 3255, Shortland St,
Auckland 1140, NZ or email: childrensbooks@hachette.co.nz

**Don't forget to include your name and address.
Only one entry per child.**

Good luck!

Fight the Beasts,
Fear the Magic

www.beastquest.co.uk

Have you checked out the Beast Quest website?
It's the place to go for games, downloads, activities,
sneak previews and lots of fun!

You can read all about your favourite beasts,
download free screensavers and desktop wallpapers
for your computer, and even challenge your friends
to a Beast Tournament.

Sign up to the newsletter at www.beastquest.co.uk
to receive exclusive extra content and the
opportunity to enter special members-only
competitions. We'll send you up-to-date info on all
the Beast Quest books, including the next exciting
series which features four brand-new Beasts!

Beast Quest®

Ferno the Fire Dragon
978 1 84616 483 5

Sepron the Sea Serpent
978 1 84616 482 8

Arcta the Mountain Giant
978 1 84616 484 2

Tagus the Horse-Man
978 1 84616 486 6

Nanook the Snow Monster
978 1 84616 485 9

Epos the Flame Bird
978 1 84616 487 3

All books priced at £4.99.
Special bumper editions priced at £5.99.

Orchard Books are available from all good bookshops, or can
be ordered from our website: www.orchardbooks.co.uk,
or telephone 01235 827702, or fax 01235 8227703.